SNATCHED

Asmaa Hussein

Illustrated by Sviatoslav Diachyk

Omar waited outside his apartment building. The school minibus had dropped him at a nearby street corner. Soon Mama would come back from buying fresh bread at the Fatih bakery. She always stopped there after work.

Usually the doorman, Amo Mohamed, would let Omar into the building. But today his old plastic lawn chair sat empty.

Omar noticed a glass of tea sitting on the small stool that the doorman used as a table. Soft streaks of steam floated from its surface. In a shiny round plate next to the tea sat a piece of baqlawa.

Its outer layer glistened in the sunlight. It was Tant Shaima's homemade baqlawa. She was the doorman's wife, and her baqlawa was famously yummy.

Omar's tummy grumbled.

Without thinking, he stretched his hand out and grabbed it. It dripped gooey, sugary goodness onto his fingers. He crammed it into his mouth and swallowed hard, before he was even able to chew all the pistachio bits properly.

He wiped his hands on his school uniform pants and let out a syrupy burp.

Omar heard footsteps approaching, so he ran behind the corner of the building to hide. He secretly watched as Amo Mohamed sat down and picked up his tea.

Uh oh.

"Shaima!" Amo Mohamed called. "Where is my baqlawa? It was right here."

She poked her head out of the open window. "I put the last piece of baqlawa right in that plate, habibi."

Amo Mohamed scratched his head. "Maybe Mishmish snatched it. Pesky cat."

Amo Mohamed sometimes fed the neighbourhood's stray cats. His favourite was a pretty tabby that he called Mishmish.

"Omar?" His mom's voice startled him. "Are you spying on someone?"

He jumped. "Oh! No, I was just waiting for you!"

Amo Mohamed spotted them walking towards the entrance and leapt out of his chair to open the door for them. "Assalaamu alaikum!"

"Walaikum assalaam," Omar replied sheepishly, sprinting towards the elevator.

GURGLE, went Omar's tummy at the dinner table. He was famished, and it took him about three minutes to empty his plate. Fried chicken and cumin-spiced lentil soup. Yum!

"Alhamdulillah." He patted his satisfied belly with both hands.

In the morning, Omar and his mom headed out early. As they got off the elevator in the lobby, they heard Amo Mohamed's voice outside. He sounded angry!

"Go away! I feed you and then you come steal my food? I don't think so!"

Who is he yelling at? Omar wondered. He pushed the door open and looked around. In the distance, Mishmish slinked away.

"Baqlawa-stealing cat..." Amo Mohamed muttered. "And don't come back!"

Omar scampered off to the minibus stop before Amo Mohamed could see him.

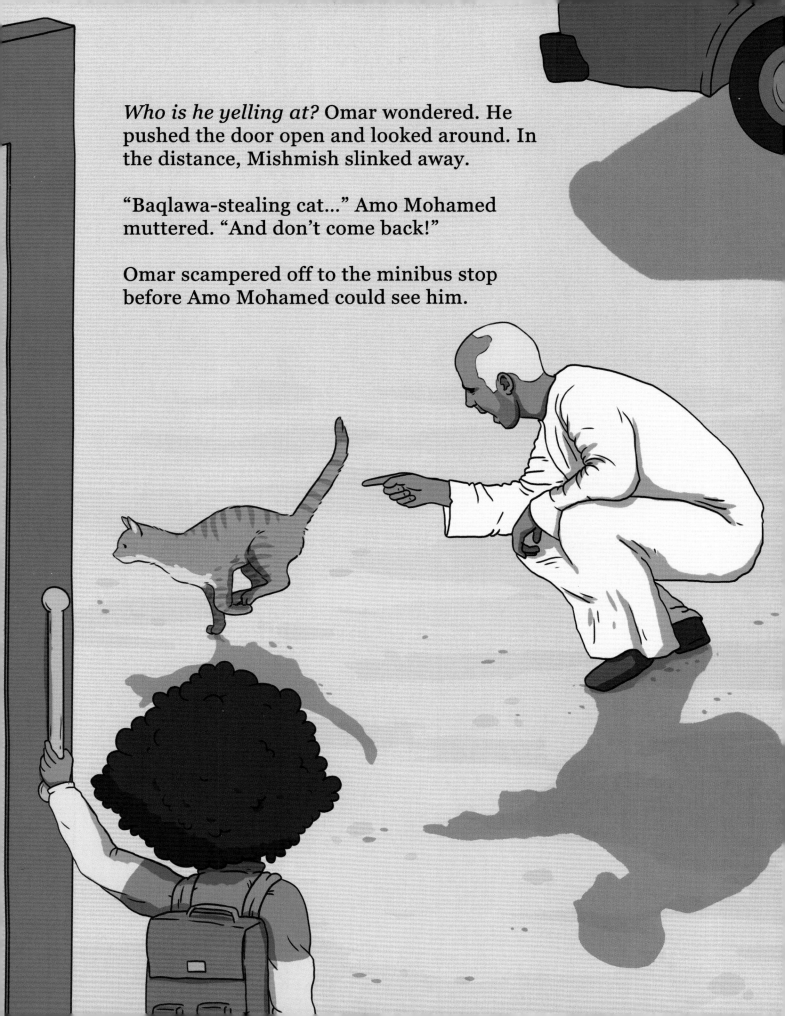

As Omar's day sped by, he felt more and more nervous about going home and facing the doorman. How would he say *Assalaamu alaikum* to Amo Mohamed every day without admitting he was the baqlawa snatcher? The pit of his stomach churned.

After school, Omar ran straight to his favourite sweet shop.

Maybe if I buy another piece of baqlawa for Amo Mohamed, I will feel better, he thought. He remembered Mama telling him that a good deed erases a bad deed.

الف مبروك

"What can I get you today, Omar?" the sweet shop owner asked.

"May I have one piece of baqlawa?"

"We ran out!" the man said. "Can I interest you in some basbousa instead?"

"No thanks," Omar mumbled.

GURGLE, went Omar's belly at the dinner table. But this gurgle was different.

"I'm not hungry. Can I go to my room?"

Mom had made chili and garlic bread. Omar's favourites!

"What's wrong?" she asked.

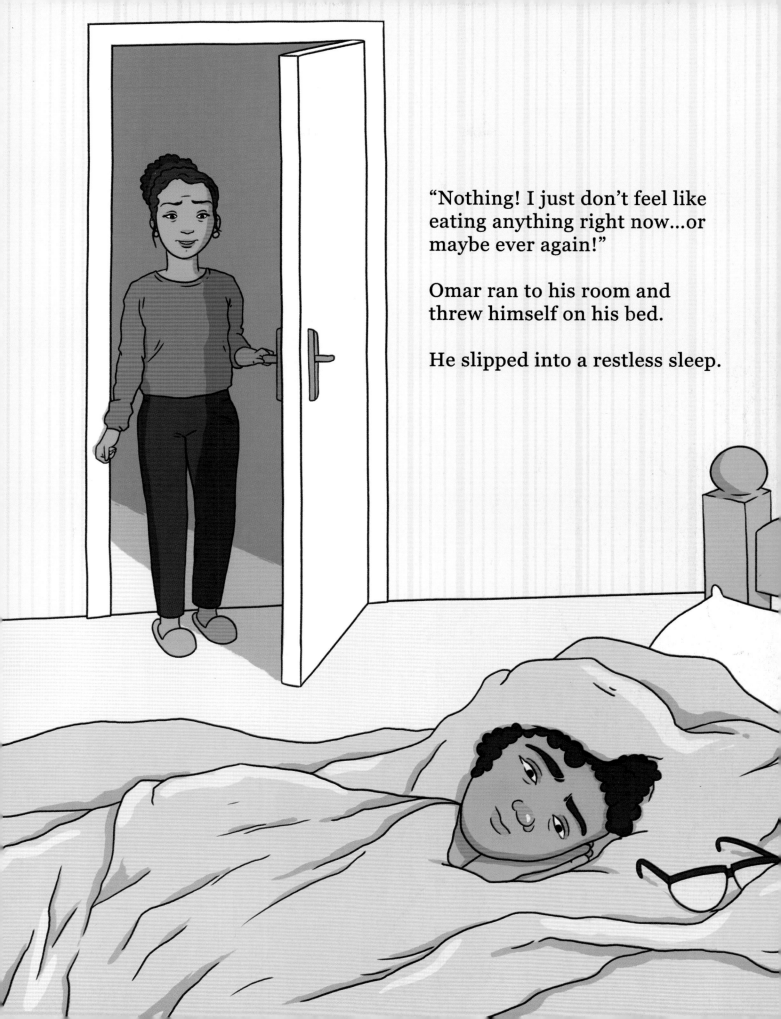

"Nothing! I just don't feel like eating anything right now...or maybe ever again!"

Omar ran to his room and threw himself on his bed.

He slipped into a restless sleep.

Omar dreamt he was walking towards the minibus stop when it started to rain. He touched the first raindrop that landed on the tip of his nose. It wasn't water – it was sticky syrup!

Chunks of baqlawa began dropping from the sky. They fell into piles on the street, bouncing off Omar's head on the way down.

"Ouch!" he yelped. "That hurts!"

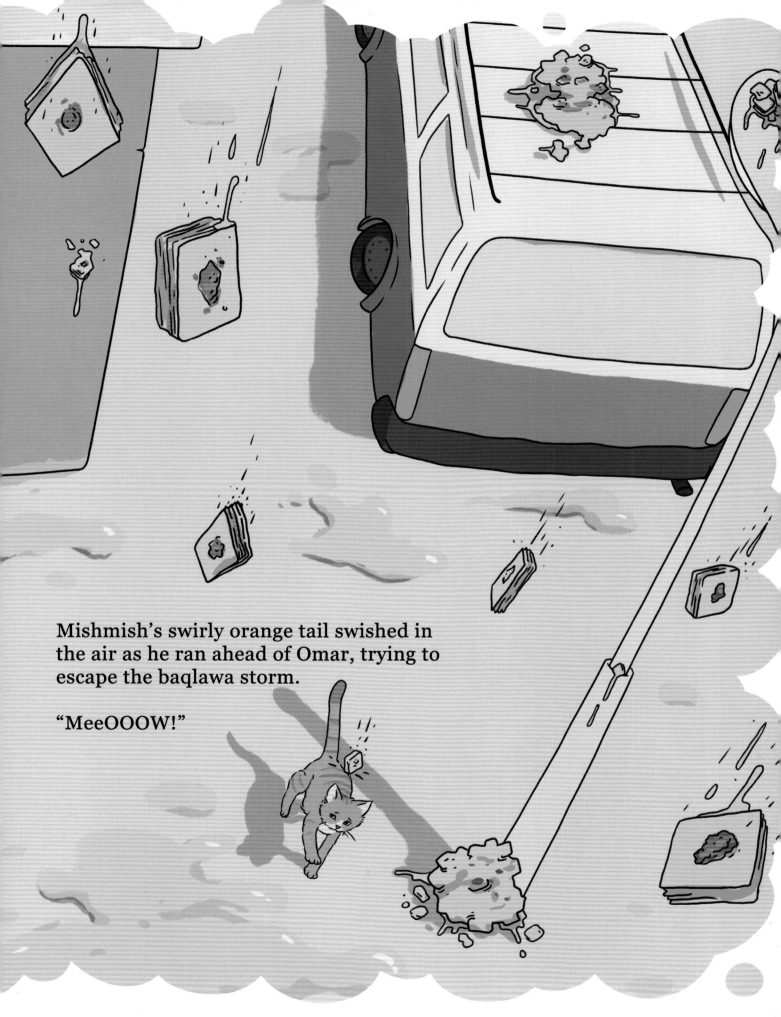

Mishmish's swirly orange tail swished in the air as he ran ahead of Omar, trying to escape the baqlawa storm.

"MeeOOOW!"

Omar woke up with a start. He was sweaty and his heart was thumping hard.

Tak tak tak! something thumped against his window.

Omar raced out of his room.

"Mama! It's raining baqlawa!"

"Baqlawa?" Mom said. "It's hail, Omar! It's a good old Egyptian winter storm – you've seen them before."

"Oh yeah..." Omar stammered. He felt a little silly for thinking pastries were falling from the sky.

"Okay, time to tell me what's going on," Mom said.

Omar sighed. "I ate something that didn't belong to me," he said. Then the rest of the story tumbled out.

Mama listened attentively. "Making mistakes is normal," she said finally. "The important thing is figuring out how to fix them."

She walked into
the kitchen with Omar trailing
behind her. She started grabbing ingredients
and setting them out on the counter: sugar, walnuts,
shredded coconut, cinnamon, butter, and a package of filo pastry.

"We're making baqlawa!"

FILO

Omar spread the filo sheets onto a baking pan and cut thin slices of butter. Mama crushed the walnuts with a rolling pin, then mixed them with sugar, cinnamon, and shredded coconut.

They carefully layered the filo sheets, nut filling, and butter, one on top of the other.

A sudden call from the muezzin startled Omar as he pushed the baking pan into the hot oven. It was already time for isha prayer.

When they finished their evening prayers, Omar and his mom pulled the baqlawa out of the oven and drowned it in sweet, rosewater-flavoured syrup. Omar fell asleep to the warm, sugary scent in their apartment.

It was nearly noon when Omar finally awoke and found his mom typing away on her laptop at the dining room table.

"Good, you're up!" she said. "Time to talk to Amo Mohamed."

"Do we have to *right now*?" Omar asked. Admitting what he did was going to be embarrassing.

"Yes," she said. "Now."

Mama had cut the baqlawa into diamond-shaped pieces. Omar picked out the ones that looked the most gooey and delicious, put them on a nice plate, and covered them with foil.

Mama and Omar headed into the lobby to find Amo Mohamed. Omar felt beads of sweat trickle down the side of his face.

What will Amo Mohamed say? Will he be very angry?

He heard Amo Mohamed humming outside. Omar looked at his mom. She nodded and gave him a gentle nudge. "We made the baqlawa together, but you have to talk to Amo Mohamed on your own."

Outside the building, Omar found Amo Mohamed sipping a cup of tea. His balding head glistened in the sunlight.

"Omar, my boy!" Amo Mohamed motioned for him to come over. "How are you today?"

"I'm fine," stammered Omar.

"What do you have there?" Amo Mohamed asked.

"This is baqlawa that I made for you."
Omar gulped and held out the plate.
"I'm the one who ate your baqlawa, not
Mishmish. I'm sorry."

Amo Mohamed took the plate.

Omar waited. *Is he
angry? Will he call
me "pesky" like
Mishmish?*

Amo Mohamed let out a great big laugh and slapped his knee. He squeezed Omar's shoulder. "It took a lot of courage to tell me the truth, and I'm proud of you. But maybe next time if you'd like a piece, just ask!"

Amo Mohamed pulled the foil back and counted the pieces of baqlawa. "I lost one piece of baqlawa and got seven instead!" he said. "Alhamdulillah."

Omar laughed along, feeling relieved.

"Biss, biss, biss," Amo Mohamed whispered. It was the sound he made whenever he wanted to call Mishmish.

Mishmish came running out of the bushes.

"I'm sorry I blamed you, my little friend," Amo Mohamed said. He broke off a tiny piece of the sugary treat for Mishmish, then let her lick the syrup off his fingers.

Mama came up behind
Omar, tousling his hair.
Amo Mohamed insisted
on sharing a piece of baqlawa
with each of them.

When the muezzin's strong,
smooth voice beckoned them
to the afternoon prayer, Omar and his
mom walked to the nearby mosque.
Their fingers were sticky and their hearts
happy.

Prophet Muhammad (peace be upon him) said,

"Be conscious of God wherever you are. Follow the bad deed with a good one to erase it, and engage others with beautiful character."

Glossary of terms

Amo:
The Arabic word for "Uncle," often used as a term of respect when referring to an older man.

Tant:
The Arabic word for "Aunt," often used as a term of respect when referring to an older woman.

Habibi:
The Arabic word for "my love."

Assalaamu alaikum:
The greetings Muslims use when they meet one another, meaning, "Peace be upon you."

Walaikum assalaam:
The response given when addressed with the Muslim greeting, meaning, "and upon you be peace."

Alhamdulillah:
A phrase used to thank God, meaning, "All praise is due to God."

Muezzin:
A person appointed to recite the call to prayer in the mosque before each of the five daily prayers.

Isha:
One of the five daily prayers a Muslim must perform.